FLYING THRU WITH GRA'MA

by Jeff McCarthy

edited by Gorica Hadzic

Denny and his Gra'ma Tina are both quite tall. In fact, Gra'ma Tina is 6 feet tall.

"Five feet twelve inches" she says with a little smile.

It runs in the family. In two weeks, Denny will be nine years old and likes to whack the top of the doorway as he passes from room to room. He dreams of the day he can do it without jumping.

Gra'ma Tina says Denny is an old soul with long legs.

"Those legs have got to travel the world, kiddo. Egypt, Thailand, Uzbekistan. The world is your oyster with legs like those."

Denny smiled and ran out back. The smell of sage stopped him in his tracks. So familiar. So pleasant. He wondered - what do kids smell when they run out into the afternoon sun, in say...Turkey?

Denny was still thinking about the wide world when, the next morning at recess, he overheard an older boy say that if you dug straight through the earth you would end up in China.

"Lots of kids have tried." the kid explained. "But, so far, nobody's made it."

China? What is in China, exactly? Denny wondered. And isn't the center of the earth made of fire? Who cares, he thought, watching a cloud in the shape of a paper lantern scud by.

As Denny ran home from school, he decided he would be the first kid in history to do it.

"I'm gonna dig to China."

He did his homework then ran to the garage. Got a shovel - and ran like a shot out back. He chose the perfect spot where the ground was soft near the pepper tree and started digging. It was getting dark but he didn't care - Denny wanted to dig.

From the house, Gra'ma Tina called out "Denny? Dinner's on the table!"

"Not hungry" Denny mumbled and kept digging.

Gra'ma Tina flipped on the flood light and came out onto the back porch. Denny hoisted another shovelful of dirt out of the hole.

"What're you doing, kid?"

"Digging to China."

She watched for a minute, smiling. Denny had found a new project.

"Hey…you know, there's an easier way to do that."

"Whoo - oo!" Denny hollered. "It's gettin' all watery down here! Gra'ma, is this Chinese water?"

"Hey Den?"

"Yeah?"

"Ever seen one of these?" Gra'ma Tina pulled something from the pocket of her apron.

"Whew! OK. Guess I'm done for now, but - man, I sure love dirt! "

Denny climbed out of the hole, nodding toward what looked like a coin that Gra'ma was holding in the palm of her hand.

"What is that?"

"Ying bi."

"What is ying bi?"

"A Chinese penny."

"Where'd you get it?"

"China. Toss it in the hole and see what happens".

"Why? What'll happen?"

"Have to wait till tomorrow to find out."

"Why? What do you mean?"

"You just do."

She saw a little hesitation in Denny's face.

"Ok... but you throw it, Gra'ma."

Gra'ma Tina came down the steps, closer to the hole.

"Alrighty - yee uhr sahn. One two three. Say it with me - yee uhr sahn."

With her, Denny said the first words he had ever spoken in Chinese.

"Yee uhr sahn. Yee uhr sahn."

Gra'ma gave the coin a little flip. Together they watched it disappear into the muddy puddle at the bottom of the hole.

"Okay…now what?"

"Now you wait."

Gra'ma put her arm around Denny and together they headed toward the porch. A firefly buzzed past.

As Gra'ma opened the screen door, Denny turned to take one last look at the hole in the darkening yard

✳ ✳ ✳ ✳ ✳ ✳ ✳ ✳ ✳ ✳

Denny was asleep maybe an hour when the breeze rustled the leaves against his bedroom window. His eyes popped open, wide awake.

He whispered to himself "…Chinese penny." He knew even the sound of tossing back the sheets could alert Gra'ma Tina. Slowly, Denny's toes reached for the floor.

The hallway light was still on. He thought to himself - there's her door, wide open. If she catches me, I'm just getting a drink. From the fridge. Ice water.

She was reading as Denny slipped past, making his way toward the back door. He crossed the cold kitchen floor then silently, turned the knob and stepped out, leaving the door ajar.

The October crickets were in full bloom as Denny crossed the yard, his long shadow leading the way.

There it was, no longer just a hole - but a still pool of water reflecting the full moon.

Reaching with his toes, he tapped the water's surface...

"...Warm." he said quietly to himself.

His reflection rippled in the puddle - when suddenly the porch light flooded the backyard...

"Young man, you need to get back to..."

STARTLED! He lost his balance, slipped, and with hardly a sound - disappeared into the water!

"Oh dear!" Gra'ma Tina blurted out as she ran across the yard.

She held her nose, counted "Yee uhr sahn..." and jumped - following Denny deep into the hole of water.

* * * * * * * * *

Down, down into the tunnel of water Denny flew...

"Gra'maaaaa!"

Into the pitch-black he sailed - vacuumed toward the center of the earth.

But the liquid rushing past was warm and strangely comforting. Was this a dream?

Denny felt the pounding of his heart, slowing - when, out of nowhere, a swarm of beautiful glowing butterflies raced up toward him…

Or were they parakeets?

Or both? Hundreds of them seemed to morph and change direction, guiding him on. Surrounded, he felt strangely protected by these pretty creatures.

Suddenly, Denny felt a tug on his foot. Leaning into his left shoulder - he flipped himself around. Pulled backwards through the tunnel, he saw a face come rushing up toward him...

Gra'ma Tina!

She reached for Denny's hand and taking it, flipped him onto her back.

Another flock of parakeets came racing past and took a sharp right down a different tunnel. Denny held on tight as Gra'ma Tina, with the boy on her back, gave a quick nod and whoosh! Away they went in the opposite direction.

Who knows how long they travelled? Time meant nothing as they flew along.

Finally, the tunnel headed straight up toward the light as a flood of soft, fragrant flowers fell toward them, welcoming Gra'ma and Denny to their destination...

And there they were - standing in a large puddle with delicate flowers floating at their feet.

Gra'ma Tina blinked, looked around and asked "So...where are we?"

Denny looked up at Gra'ma, waiting for an answer. But he could wait no longer and exploded with questions...

"Whoa! That was amazing! How did we do-?"

"Ssshhhh..."

"But that was the most-"

"Yes, I know. But quiet, love. Just look and listen."

"And what were those little…?"

"Sssshhhh"

Gra'ma Tina gently stroked his hair as she looked out at the mountains. Denny could tell from the look in her eyes - this was familiar territory. He took a deep breath and looked around.

There they stood at the foot of Huangshan mountains with the rare, late afternoon moon smiling down on them.

Suddenly, an arrow whizzed overhead - landing silently in the grass several yards away. And then another, a bit closer. As Gra'ma Tina reached for Denny's hand, a voice came from behind...

"My friends! The children are practicing. Not safe. Come with me."

An old Chinese man had taken Gra'ma's hand and quickly lead them toward a stand of pine trees as a swarm of arrows landed behind them in the grass.

Gra'ma Tina, to Denny's surprise, spoke to the man in Chinese.

"Can you take us to Zhen Zhen?"

"What are you saying, Gra'ma?" Denny asked with great curiosity.

"One second, sweetie. Just stay close."

Gra'ma Tina listened intently to faint voices that could be heard in the near distance, when a loud cheer now exploded from within the pines.

The little man turned with a huge smile and said something that Denny didn't understand.

"He said what?"

"Denny, we are in luck! People are gathering for the Moon Festival!"

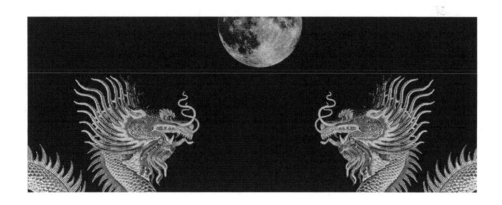

* * * * * * * * *

The man led them to a clearing in the pines where they found themselves surrounded by many families, setting up tables of food and activities for the festival.

"Tina….!"

Gra'ma and Denny turned to see a smiling, little grey haired woman coming toward them.

"For goodness sake, when did you arrive?"

"Oh! my dear Zhen Zhen! How are you? We came thru just a few minutes ago" said Gra'ma Tina, bending over and hugging her.

"Well, perfect timing!" exclaimed Zhen Zhen. "The children's procession and hanging of the sun lanterns is about to begin!"

"Zhen Zhen, I'd like you to meet my grandson, Denny."

Denny stood there smiling, he and Gra'ma Tina towering over everyone.

"I have waited years to meet you, young man. My goodness - he's so tall, Tina… like you! My grandson, Liang, is here too - somewhere, with his bow and arrow."

Denny followed Gra'ma Tina and her friend, awed by all that was happening. Down the hill, he noticed a boy about his age kneeling and drawing with a stick in the dirt.

"Gra'ma, I'm going down there."

"Ah, yes. There he is now! My grandson, Liang." Zhen Zhen said pointing at the kneeling boy. "By all means, yes, go and introduce yourself."

"We'll be right here, kiddo."

"So, Tina - your river passage! I'm so happy to hear you're still hanging on to a few ying bi..."

"Oh yes! Just this afternoon, I discovered I had a couple left as I watched Denny start to dig."

Gra'ma Tina kissed the air over Denny's head as he started down the hill.

* * * * * * * * * *

Denny approached the kneeling boy and watched him draw with his stick in the earth.

Suddenly, a butterfly emerged and fluttered into the air. Liang continued to draw as another lifted out of the earth and flew away.

"Wow!" Denny cried, startling Liang who quickly turned to Denny.

"Sorry..." Denny said, grinning from ear to ear "...but how do you do that!?"

The boy smiled broadly up at Denny then turned back to the ground and continued drawing. This time, a small bird - a blue parakeet - came to life and flew like a shot to the limb of a nearby tree.

"That's amazing!" Denny laughed.

Liang jumped up and with the nod of his head gestured for Denny to follow him further down the hill. The boys took off walking and soon walking became running.

As they came to the edge of the woods, the boys began to compete - laughing and whooping, climbing over and under branches in a million ways.

Liang was hanging by his knees, his head a couple feet off the ground, when he pulled the drawing stick from his belt and with a few gestures in the dirt - a little raccoon came to life then ran off into the woods.

Denny laughed - then with his foot, cracked a stick from a fallen branch and quickly sketched in the dirt - the image of a pug dog. Denny stood there waiting, looking at the image. And waited some more- but nothing. Denny's pug just sat there with his curly tail.

Sitting above him on a wide branch, Liang watched Denny -- then extended his hand, offering his drawing stick.

Feeling very honored, Denny took it and knelt down again.
With a few light strokes, a nervous little field mouse appeared. Looking up at Denny - then over to Liang - the mouse squeaked and quickly disappeared into the end of a fallen log.

The boys looked at each other… then fell on the ground, laughing and enjoying the cool afternoon air.

As they finally got to their feet, they turned to head back up the hill when a low, raspy voice came from behind…

"Hold on, kid. You got my stick."

Three tough looking boys stepped out from behind a huge boulder. They approached Denny and Liang, kicking leaves out of their way.

Liang became very still, holding his ground. Denny looked to Liang, then to the rough faces of the three boys.

Liang locked eyes with the oldest, the leader.

"This doesn't belong to you."

"Hand it over. Now - or else."

Denny's heart pounded in his throat. Liang tightened his grip on the stick and shouted "Now!" as he and Denny took off tearing through the woods.

"Oh! Now they will pay!" the leader snapped. The bullies cackled and took off after them.

The threat of the older boys shot our champions full of a super energy. Bounding over rocks and logs, they cut a path to the right, heading deeper into the forest.

Behind them they heard the oldest boy order the others "Go! Go!! Catch them!"

Liang and Denny had gained some ground when Liang suddenly stopped in his tracks, his arms over his head. About thirty yards ahead...

A rushing RIVER! The overgrown woods made it clear that the only way to escape these bullies was across the water.

"Let's do it." Denny shouted as they raced to the water's edge.

Liang pulled the stick from his belt and holding it with both hands - CRACKED it in two over his leg. He handed Denny half, then got to work drawing in the air at the river's edge.

Denny watched. What could Liang possibly be drawing? But with a few strokes he had created the rungs up to a narrow footbridge! As he madly drew, the rope bridge was quickly coming to life, suspended over the river that was racing by a few feet below.

"BRILLIANT!" shouted Denny as he stepped up beside Liang. With both boys drawing now - they would quickly be to the other side.

As they drew close to the far side of the river, Denny threw a look over his shoulder to see the bullies shouting battle cries, wildly racing out onto the bridge.

Now on the other side, Denny and Liang leapt from the bridge to the ground and nodding in agreement, their sticks quickly sliced the rope bridge that had just brought them to safety. In an instant, the bullies out in the middle of the bridge flailed wildly and fell into the river.

"Help! I can't swim! I beg you!!" the leader yelled at the top of his lungs. His sidekicks weren't doing much better as the current was pulling them all downstream.

Feeling compassion for the three helpless boys that had moments earlier been terrorizing them, Liang watched as Denny knelt at the river's edge and with a few broad strokes drew a small raft - pushing it out toward the boys thrashing in the water.

Denny and Liang watched as one by one, the boys pulled themselves miserably up onto the raft that carried them all quickly downstream.

✳ ✳ ✳ ✳ ✳ ✳ ✳ ✳ ✳

The woods were now turning dark. Denny was thinking of Gra'ma Tina and knew it was time to return to the gathering at the top of the hill.

He turned to find Liang put the finishing touches on a beautiful black horse that stood glistening, ready to take them back. Denny hoisted

Liang up, then threw his long leg up over the back of the horse and the boys were mounted.

The full moon lit the way as they headed out of the woods and up the hill. The boys felt grateful for their safety and new friendship.

* * * * * * * * *

Gra'ma Tina and Zhen Zhen watched as the Moon Festival was now in full swing. In the old tradition, parents helped the children load and shoot arrows at the nine paper lanterns made to look like giant suns hanging from the trees.

"So, Tina..." Zhen Zhen explained "Legend tells us of a young man who, with bow and arrow, shoots nine of the ten suns out of the sky - leaving his wife alone on the moon, eating moon cakes. Have one. They're delicious!"

The ladies munched on moon cakes and giggled together as the festival continued on around them.

"Now that it's dark, Zhen Zhen, I'm feeling a little concerned about Denny and Liang."

"Oh, Liang knows his way very well around these mountains. And if I know Liang - he won't want to miss out on the moon cakes."

And with that, up over the rise of the hill came the boys trotting along on the horse.

"Gra'ma!" Denny shouted happily as he jumped down.

"Where did you two disappear?" Gra'ma Tina asked.

Denny and Liang looked at each other and grinned. "Oh...just a little adventure!"

"Well, kiddo, we need to think about heading home while the night is still young!"

Gra'ma Tina wrapped her arm around Denny but he was focused on the last remaining sun - as the village kid's arrows kept sailing past the lantern, disappearing into the dark.

"My friend..." Liang handed Denny a bow and arrow and led him to the front of the crowd. Drawing the arrow, Denny carefully aimed at the last glowing paper sun hanging from the tree.

He released the arrow and...THWACK!!! ripped through the paper lantern - leaving only the full moon, throbbing overhead in the night sky.

The families cheered as Denny turned to Gra'ma Tina, proudly raising the bow over his head. Together they smiled and nodded, knowing it was time to head home.

✳ ✳ ✳ ✳ ✳ ✳ ✳ ✳ ✳

Gra'ma Tina pulled open the curtains. The morning sun filled the bedroom as Denny stirred from a deep sleep.

"Morning, kiddo. Rise and Shine!"

"Huh?....wha?....uh-kay."

Denny rubbed his face and slowly padded into the bathroom.

Gra'ma pulled up the bedspread as Denny reappeared in the doorway.

"Gra'ma....last night. What was that?!? A dream?"

"Dream?"

"How did you do that?"

"Do what?"

"China."

"I didn't do anything." Gra'ma Tina smiled to herself as she finished making the bed. "China has always been there - and China always will be there."

"But..." Denny walked to the window and stared out across the yard. Gra'ma Tina sat on the edge of the bed watching him. He slowly turned to her.

"Ying bi. Yee, uhr, sahn?"

"Yes. One, two, three."

Gra'ma Tina reached into her apron pocket, pulling out a handful of coins from all over the world. She held them out to Denny.

"Hey! Let's go somewhere else tonight!"

She looked into Denny's glowing face and smiled.

"You need to get ready for school right now, love. We will have plenty of adventures down the road." With that, Gra'ma Tina got up and headed down the hallway.

"But how do those coins… ?"

"Your breakfast is waiting, kiddo."

Denny stood there quietly for a minute, smiling, looking out onto the beautiful bright morning.

As he headed toward the kitchen, Denny reached up and without jumping - whacked the top of the doorway.

The End

Never Give Up

Made in the USA
Las Vegas, NV
25 April 2022

47964927R00015